Sammy and the Pecan Pie

SEAN COVEY

Illustrated by Stacy Curtis

Ready-to-Read

Simon Spotlight

New York   London   Toronto   Sydney   New Delhi

To my intelligent and abundant son Nathan
who has always been a best friend
to his little brother, Weston
—Sean Covey

For my twin brother, Tracy
—Stacy Curtis

SIMON SPOTLIGHT
An imprint of Simon & Schuster Children's Publishing Division
1230 Avenue of the Americas, New York, New York 10020
This Simon Spotlight edition December 2019
Copyright © 2013 by Franklin Covey Co.
For information about special discounts for bulk purchases, please contact Simon & Schuster Special
Sales at 1-866-506-1949 or business@simonandschuster.com.
Manufactured in the United States of America 1119 LAK
2 4 6 8 10 9 7 5 3 1
CIP data for this book is available from the Library of Congress.
ISBN 978-1-5344-4454-6 (hc)
ISBN 978-1-5344-4453-9 (pbk)
ISBN 978-1-5344-4455-3 (eBook)

Sammy and his twin sister, Sophie,
usually got along.
Sometimes he wished she didn't
do everything right.
One day at school,
Ms. Hoot announced that Sophie got
one hundred percent on her test.
It wasn't the first time.

"You did a good job too, Sammy,"
said Jumper.
Still Sammy was not happy.

Sammy wished he could get
all the correct answers like Sophie.

Ms. Hoot was happy.
All her students tried their best.
The bell rang and school was over.

The gang went
to Mandy's Candies after school.
They rewarded themselves
for doing so well on the test.

"We have four dollars and fifty cents.
How much candy can we get?"
asked Lily Skunk.
"We can get three bags of yummy
gummies, two chocolate worms,
and two lucky suckers," said Sophie.

They paid for the candy
and went to the park.
"Wow, Sophie, you added that up
fast," said Goob.
"Yeah, your brain must be huge,"
said Jumper. "Like as big as a
basketball."

Tagalong Allie asked Sammy what it
was like to have such a smart sister.
Sammy shrugged.
"I guess it's all right," he said
as he headed home.

Later that night Sammy and Sophie
were with their mom and dad.
Sophie told them about
the upcoming spelling bee.

"How about you, Sammy?
Are you going to enter?" asked Mom.
"I guess," Sammy mumbled.
Deep down, he expected
Sophie would win.
Soon it was time for dinner.

After dinner Mom served
the special dessert she had made.
It was pecan pie—Sammy's favorite.
She placed pie slices
on everyone's plates.

Sammy compared
his plate with Sophie's.
Her piece of pie seemed bigger
than the one on his plate.
"Why does Sophie always get the
bigger piece? She always wins!"
yelled Sammy.

Sammy ran to his room
and slammed the door.
His mom followed him.

Sammy was laying on the floor
when Mom entered his room.
Mom asked Sammy
what was bothering him.

"It's just that Sophie gets all the attention. Everyone thinks she's so smart. And it makes me feel dumb," said Sammy.

"I'm sorry you feel that way, Sammy. But you're smart too!" said Mom.

"I never get all the correct answers
on my spelling tests," said Sammy.
"Maybe not, but Sophie can't build
model rockets like you can,"
said Mom. "Just because Sophie
is good at something doesn't take
anything away from you."

"What do you mean?" asked Sammy.
"Well, some people think that life is
like a pie," Mom began.
"If someone gets a big piece, there
is less for you. But really, life is
more like an all-you-can-eat buffet.
Everyone can have all the pie they
want. Sophie can have a big piece,
and so can you. You can both win."

A few days later it was time
for the big science fair.
Everyone was excited.
Tagalong Allie took pictures
of all the booths.

"Hey, everyone," hollered Sophie. "Come take a look at Sammy's booth! It's phenomenal!"

"Thanks, Sophie," said Sammy. "Yours is good too."

Just then Sammy was given a ribbon. He won first prize! Sammy blushed as Sophie beamed.

"The science fair was a blast today.
Let's go home and see if
Mom has some pie left,"
said Sammy as they walked home.
"Yeah, as long as I get the biggest
piece," said Sophie,
winking at Sammy.
"I think there's more than enough
for both of us," said Sammy.
"Last one home's a rotten egg!"

The twins raced home and laughed
the entire time.

Up for Discussion

1. After Sophie got all the answers correct on her test, how did Sammy feel?

2. Of all the candy in Mandy's Candies, which would you like the best?

3. Why did Sammy unhappily leave the table after dinner? What did his mother say to make him feel better?

4. What did Sammy make for the science fair?

5. How did Sophie feel about Sammy doing so well at the science fair? How should you feel when one of your brothers or sisters or friends do well at something?

Baby Steps

1. Draw a picture of something your friend is really good at. Now draw a picture of something you're really good at.
2. Do you ever compare yourself to another person? Who is it? Talk to your parents about that.
3. Play a game and don't worry about who wins or loses. Play just for the fun of it.
4. Help a family member do a household chore. Work together to make it go faster.
5. Compliment a family member on something they do well.

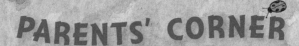

PARENTS' CORNER

HABIT ④ —Think Win-Win: *Everyone Can Win*

I adore my two little boys, Nathan and Weston. They are three years apart and they are the best of friends. I'm especially proud of the way they attend each other's sports events to cheer each other on. Becoming jealous of each other's success never even enters their minds. As far as they're concerned, if one of them succeeds, they both succeed. This is the win-win spirit, the belief that there is more than enough success to go around and to spare.

I hope my boys will always feel this way toward each other and their friends. But I know this won't be easy in this competitive world of ours. As we mature, if we aren't careful, envy and jealousy can creep into our hearts. And it is not uncommon to find ourselves becoming threatened by the successes of others, especially those closest to us, as if their success somehow takes something away from us.

As parents and teachers, there is so much we can do to instill confidence and win-win thinking in our kids. First, we can show unconditional love at all times instead of doling out love based on performance. Next, we can avoid comparative language, such as "Why can't you do your homework like your brother?" In its place we can use language that affirms a child's worth and potential, such as "You're so good at that!" or "I'm happy to see that you tried your very hardest."

In this story, point out that, like Sammy, we too need to learn to not be jealous or to compare ourselves to others. The truth is, we are all VIPs. There is something different and special inside of each of us.